REDNECK NIGHT BEFORE CHRISTMAS

REDNECK NIGHT BEFORE CHRISTMAS

Written by David Davis
Illustrated by James Rice

PELICAN PUBLISHING COMPANY
Gretna 1997

To Laurel and Hardy, who first taught me how to laugh, and to my wife, Leanne,
who sacrificed much, so I could try to be funny

The word "Pelican" and the depiction of a pelican are trademarks
of Pelican Publishing Company, Inc., and are registered
in the U.S. Patent and Trademark Office.

Library of Congress Cataloging-in-Publication Data

Davis, David (David R.), 1948-
  Redneck night before Christmas / written by David Davis ;
illustrated by James Rice.
    p. cm.
  Summary: Presents a redneck twist on the well-known poem about an
important Christmas visitor, who arives in a pickup truck
accompanied by eight hound dogs.
  ISBN 1-56554-293-2 (alk. paper)
  1. Rednecks—Juvenile poetry. 2. Christmas—Juvenile poetry.
3. Santa Claus—Juvenile poetry. 4. Children's poetry, American.
[1. Santa Claus—Poetry. 2. Christmas—Poetry. 3. American poetry.
4. Narrative poetry.] I. Rice, James, 1934-   ill. II. Title.
PS3554.A93344R43 1997
811'.54—dc21   97-14421
                                                           CIP
                                                           AC

Printed in Hong Kong

Published by Pelican Publishing Company, Inc.
1101 Monroe Street, Gretna, LA 70053

REDNECK NIGHT BEFORE CHRISTMAS

On the evenin' 'fore Christmas, in our mobile house
Nothing was movin' (I had blasted the mouse).
We couldn't hang stockings in our trailer home here,
'Cause we don't wear socks the rest of the year.

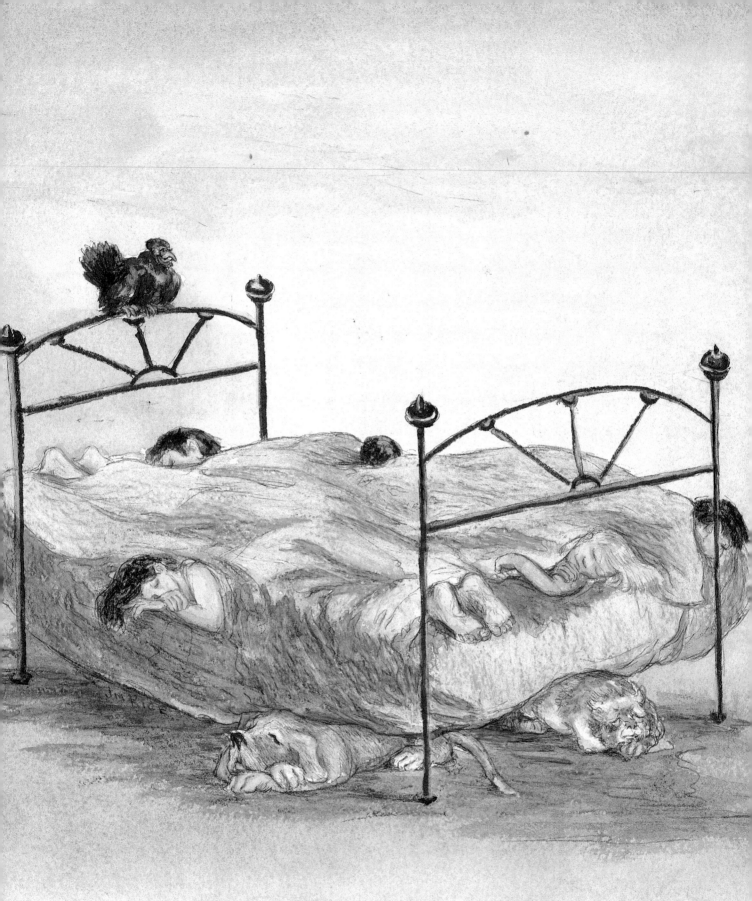

The rug-rats wuz out cold in their feather beds.
There'd been a big tussle, and they'd skinned up their heads.

Maw smeared on her cold cream, and I spit out my chews.
We'd stayed up too late—and we needed a snooze.

When out in the yard I heard such a clamor,
Thought the laws had come back to put me in the slammer.
Away to the window I went at a run,
Poked a hole in the plastic and pointed my gun.

The bug light a-shining on the new-fallen snow
Gave the brightness of day to our pickups below,
When, what with my bloodshot old eyes did I see,
A Ford-load a' dogs, a-coming at me,

With a little old driver, I thought what the heck!
It was, without doubt, the Christmas Redneck!

All around the truck the hound dawgs they came,
And he hollered, and shouted, and called them by name:

"Now, Bugler! now, Jughead! now, Fiddler and Shepherd!
On, Yeller! on, Smoky! on, Blue Tick and Leopard!
To the top of the steps, to the trailer's back wall!"
They crawled on everything, one and all.

As "coke" cans when empty out my old pickup fly,
Like a dip of old snuff, spit up to the sky,
So up to my double wide the old feller flew,
With a truck full of goods, and the hound dawgs too.

And then, in a minute, I heard and I saw
The jumping and running of each doggie's paw.

As I put down my shotgun, and was turnin' around;
Through the back door the Redneck jumped in with a bound.

In a camouflage suit, from his head to his shoes,
He moved like a feller with no time to lose.

A box full of moon pies and an RC twelve-pack,
And a deer-hunting spotlight came off of his back.

His face—how leathery! It commanded respect.
His nose was as red as the back of his neck.
The chew in his mouth drew it up like a bow,
And the white beard of his chin caught the small overflow.

On the front of the cap, "Bless the NRA,"
And on the back of his shirt, "Go ahead, make my day."
I swiveled my head and looked down at his bag,
And there on the side was the old Southern flag.

With square jaws and shoulders, a real good ole boy—
I laughed at this specter, in pure flat-out joy;
A wink of his eye and his smilin' beneath
Showed me that his mouth was sure missing some teeth.

He spoke nary a word, but came straight to me,
And laid in my hands a brand-new CB.

Maw got a girdle to hold in her pelvis,
And a velvet painting of her idol Elvis.

He sprang to his rig as his dogs ran nearby
And whistled them up as he aimed for the sky.

As he drove out of sight, I heard him say,
"Be a good ole boy on this Christmas Day!"